D0469182

Note to parents, carers and teachers

Read it yourself is a series of modern stories, favourite characters and traditional tales written in a simple way for children who are learning to read. The books can be read independently or as part of a guided reading session.

Each book is carefully structured to include many high-frequency words vital for first reading. The sentences on each page are supported closely by pictures to help with understanding, and to offer lively details to talk about.

The books are graded into four levels that progressively introduce wider vocabulary and longer stories as a reader's ability and confidence grows.

Ideas for use

- Begin by looking through the book and talking about the pictures. Has your child heard this story before?

- Help your child with any words he does not know, either by helping him to sound them out or supplying them yourself.

- Developing readers can be concentrating so hard on the words that they sometimes don't fully grasp the meaning of what they're reading. Answering the puzzle questions on pages 30 and 31 will help with understanding.

For more information and advice on Read it yourself and book banding, visit **www.ladybird.com/readityourself**

Book
Band
6

Level 2 is ideal for children who have received some reading instruction and can read short, simple sentences with help.

Special features:

Frequent repetition of main story words and phrases

Short, simple sentences

Large, clear type

Careful match between story and pictures

It is Sports Day at school.

Peppa, George and everyone are there.

6

7

First, it is the running race.

"Ready, steady, go!" says Madame Gazelle.

They all run as fast as they can.

8

9

Educational Consultant: Geraldine Taylor
Book Banding Consultant: Kate Ruttle

LADYBIRD BOOKS

UK | USA | Canada | Ireland | Australia
India | New Zealand | South Africa

Ladybird Books is part of the Penguin Random House group of companies
whose addresses can be found at global.penguinrandomhouse.com.

www.penguin.co.uk   www.puffin.co.uk   www.ladybird.co.uk

Penguin
Random House
UK

Text adapted from Sports Day, first published by Ladybird Books, 2008
This version first published by Ladybird Books, 2013
012

This book is based on the
TV Series 'Peppa Pig'
'Peppa Pig' is created by
Neville Astley and Mark Baker
Peppa Pig © Astley Baker Davies Ltd/
Entertainment One UK Ltd, 2003

www.peppapig.com

Printed in China

A CIP catalogue record for this book is
available from the British Library

ISBN: 978-0-723-27317-2

Sports Day

Written by Lorraine Horsley

It is Sports Day at school.

Peppa, George and everyone
are there.

First, it is the running race.

"Ready, steady, go!"
says Madame Gazelle.

They all run as fast
as they can.

9

But Peppa is not ready.

She comes last and she
is not at all happy.

Rebecca Rabbit wins
the running race.

"Hooray!" everyone says.

Next, it is the long jump.

"Ready, steady, go!" says
Madame Gazelle again.

George jumps as far as
he can, but he comes last.

George is not happy at all.

Richard Rabbit wins
the long jump.

"Hooray!" everyone says.

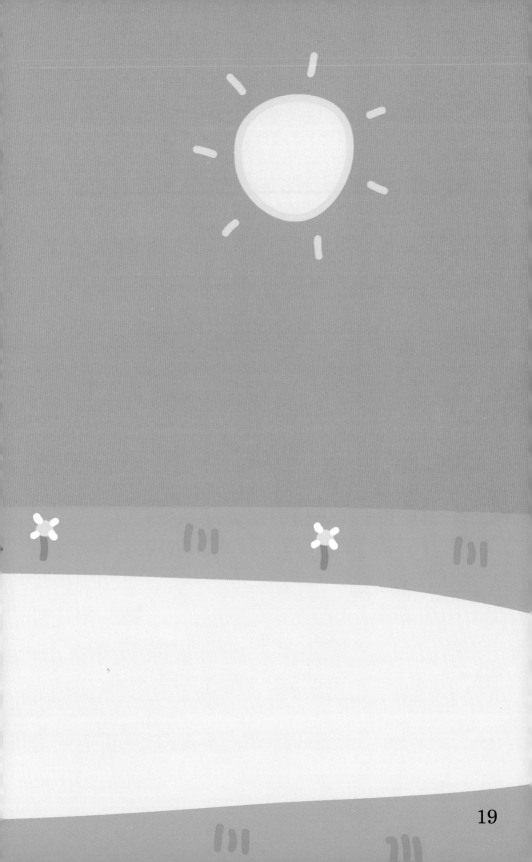

Next, it is the relay race.

"Ready, steady, go!" says
Madame Gazelle again.

Daddy Pig runs as fast
as he can.

"Here, Peppa!" says Daddy Pig. "Run as fast as you can!"

But Peppa is not ready.

Emily Elephant wins
the relay race.

"Hooray!" everyone says.

Peppa comes last again
and she is not happy at all.

Next, it is the tug of war.

"Ready, steady, go!"
says Madame Gazelle.

Everyone tugs as hard
as they can.

SNAP! The rope breaks.

"Now everyone wins!"
says Madame Gazelle.

"Hooray!" says Peppa.
"I win at last! I like
Sports Day!"

How much do you remember about Peppa Pig: Sports Day? Answer these questions and find out!

- **Who wins the running race?**

- **Who wins the long jump?**

- **Where does Peppa come in the relay race?**

- **What happens in the tug of war?**

Look at the pictures and match them to the character names.

Madame Gazelle

Emily Elephant

Rebecca Rabbit

Richard Rabbit

George

Peppa

Daddy Pig

Read it yourself with Ladybird

Tick the books you've read!

For beginner readers who can read short, simple sentences with help.

Level 2

For more confident readers who can read simple stories with help.

Level 3

The Read it yourself with Ladybird app is now available for iPad, iPhone and iPod touch

App also available on Android devices